This book is a gift of love

To _____

From _____

How Do
I Love You?

Written and Illustrated by
P. K. Hallinan

With special thanks to Pat Pingry

Ideals Children's Books • Nashville, Tennessee
an imprint of Hambleton-Hill Publishing, Inc.

Published by Ideals Children's Books
An imprint of Hambleton-Hill Publishing, Inc.
Nashville, Tennessee 37218

Printed and bound in the United States of America

ISBN 0-8249-8505-2 (pbk.)
ISBN 1-57102-112-4 (hc)

How do I love you?
Let me count the ways.

I love you on your very best...

and very worst of days.

I love to see you laughing
and dancing in the rain.

And even when you lose your shoes,
I love you just the same.

I love to hear you singing.

I love to see you smile.

I love the way you take each day
in your own unhurried style.

I'm happy when you're happy,

and I'm sorry when you're sad.

And even though it may not show,
I love you when you're bad.

How do I love you?
Well, now, let me see. . .

I love the way you act so brave
when you fall and hurt your knee.

I love to watch you sleeping,
tucked away in dreams.

I love to hear you whisper
all your giant plans and schemes.

I love the way you wear your pants
with the front part in the back

and the way you walk around sometimes
with your head inside a sack.

I love to see you deep in thought.

I love to watch you play.

And though I'm sure you'll never know,
I love you more each day.

How do I love you?
It's impossible to say.

For if I had a million days
and time enough for all the praise,
I couldn't tell you all the ways. . .

I love you.